Samuel Willoughby Duffield

Eric or the Fall of a Crown

Samuel Willoughby Duffield

Eric or the Fall of a Crown

ISBN/EAN: 9783337282035

Printed in Europe, USA, Canada, Australia, Japan

Cover: Foto ©Andreas Hilbeck / pixelio.de

More available books at **www.hansebooks.com**

ERIC:

OR THE

FALL OF A CROWN.

———

Privately Printed for

THE AUBURN READING CIRCLE.

1878.

PROEM.

This story, like a fair Pompeian lamp —
   Its bronze time-eaten and its oil long spent —
   I fill again, remembering how it went
Of old in Beauty's hand, through gloom and damp
Of prison corridors.

                Our spirits cramp
   Too often when in such strict confines bent;
Too often, at our best, we but revamp
   Old fabrics, fill old lamps.

                  To this extent,
At least, I ask you, bear with such a theme.
   A royal garment and a royal light
I bring you, worthy of no faint esteem
   If once their meaning strike upon your sight;
For we ourselves are patterns of a dream
   And need equipment for this earth's long night.

S. A. W. D.

DRAMATIS PERSONÆ.

ERIC XIV., *King of Sweden; son of Gustavus Vasa.*

COUNT SVENTE STURE, *an old Counselor.*

BURRÆUS,
GORAN PERSSON, } *Tutors and Advisers to the King.*

PRINCE JOHN,
PRINCE CHARLES, } *Half-brothers to Eric; created Dukes by Gustavus.*

LARS LARSON, *a Jester and Troubadour.*

STEN LEYONHUFWUD, *Sergeant of the Guard.*

CATHERINE MONE, *Wife to Eric.*

1ST WOMAN.

2D WOMAN.

3D WOMAN.

A Servant, a Jailor, a Priest, Attendants, &c.

SCENE. — *Mostly in Stockholm, except in the last act of the play.*

TIME. — *Between* 1560 *and* 1566, *A. D.*

ERIC:

OR THE

FALL OF A CROWN.

ACT I.

SCENE I. — *Stockholm.   The public square.*

(*Enter* 1ST *and* 2D WOMEN, *and* LARS.)

1st W. They will keep us here all the day, these nobles! One would think they had nothing to do but to make people wait!

2d W. Softly, mother; it is not so short a distance to Upsala, that they can journey it thus soon. Is it, Lars?

Lars. Patience, ladies, is an ox that chews the cud. Be very patient, therefore, and ruminate on this matter. It is the manner of your sex to be silent. A still tongue makes a steady brain, as Jan Svenson said when he came home from the tavern.

2d. W. That is said unkindly, Lars Larson.

Lars. Oh, well now, if you are to be vexed about it, that will give you something to think of until the procession comes. A mind without occupation is like a cat without a ball of yarn. Roll the subject over and over, ladies, and perhaps you will make a pretty tangle of it by afternoon. No; for me Sweden is not yet the land of the troubadours.

2d W. Who are the troubadours, then?

Lars. Singers of sweet songs and players on the

lute; living in warm, lovely air; cheering the hearts of beautiful ladies — like yourselves; only, the ladies never grew angry at a jest.

1st W. We are not angry, Lars, but we have stood and sat and strolled around this square all the morning. Now there is the dinner to cook and the house to clean, and the days are now good, and it is fit that hard working people should be using this fine summer weather.

2d W. They say the new king quarrels with his brothers.

1st W. So he does. He told the old father Gustavus that to give Prince John and Prince Charles so much power was to make trouble for the kingdom. Truly, Eric, himself, will trouble it. Come hither, Gossip!

(*Enter* 3D WOMAN.)

What was it the physician said when Eric was born?

3d W. What did he say?

Lars. Yes; what did he say? never mind me; I'm a perfect old woman myself, and I like to hear stories.

3d W. What did he say?

1st and 2d W. Come! what did he say?

3d W. Let me see. Thirty years ago it was — yes, it was thirty years. That was when Christine was a baby. You know Christine — she married a miner in Dalecarlia. Aye; those were brave men, those miners. How they fought for Gustavus Vasa!

1st W. Spare us that, Gossip. That was when you and I were young and good-looking. Tell us the story.

3d W. About Eric — yes, about Eric — but I was not young and good-looking any more than you were; and we have both passed three-score.

2d W. We live near enough to settle that point like neighbors, to-morrow. Tell us the story. I never heard it. I know it must be something dreadful, for the whole square looks as gloomy as a funeral.

Lars. Certainly, tell us the story. I can sing it to my lute some day and when I am famous, you will be able to say, We helped to make that poet! Oh, yes; of course, tell us the story.

3d W. Master Lars Larson, I knew your father and your mother. They were sensible folk and never went capering over Europe with a fiddle in a bag. Now my daughter Christine's husband's brother's son is such another. He was born the same day as Prince Eric — more's the sorrow. Do you suppose this procession will ever arrive?

1st W. I remember that you told me that your aunt —

3d W. No; it was my sister —

1st W. Was nurse maid to Queen Margaret —

3d W. I tell you it was Queen Catherine —

1st W. And when she was there, Prince Eric was two days old.

3d W. What lies! he was not yet born. Three days the doctors waited; that was nearly as bad as my daughter Christine. Says the old doctor —

1st W. If he is as long being born as his grandmother is in telling a story —

3d W. Do you think I will be insulted by you, Lura Pedersen! God send you a civiler tongue!

(*Going.*)

Lars. Stay a moment, madam, and suffer your most dutiful and obedient servant to entreat you, in the humblest manner, to favor us with the continuation of your pathetic recital.

3d W. Bless me, Lars Larson, who could think you had learned such fine phrases in France and Italy. Dear,

dear, and I knew your father when he was a mere slip
of a lad, and a better fashioned man than you are. I
warrant me, that no doctors said about him, "Let him
not be born for he is a child of sorrow to the land." No,
no ; he was a good man and he taught his son good
manners.

1*st* W. Go on with the story, Gossip.

2*d* W. Do go on with the story. See how black
and troubled are the people's faces. Men say Prince
Eric is a cruel and haughty man. Do tell us what the
doctors said.

3*d* W. I'll never tell ye. I promised never to tell.
There ! say no more to me. See, the North Gate opens
and the procession comes in. Where can that Nils be ?
The urchin ! I must go and find him.

(*Exit.*)

1*st* W. Perhaps she told us after all what the doctors
said.

2*d* W. There has always been a strange idea that
Prince Eric was to be a bad king.

1*st* W. Let us stand here by this pillar and see him
as he passes.

(*They step aside.*)

ACT I.

SCENE II. — *Same place.   Procession approaching.*

LARS *stands alone.*

Lars. —

This is like Italy ! The sky is clear ;   ..
Birds sing and music sounds and horses prance.
Heralds and knights and nobles — see them go !
And these, who are they ? Princes ? By their dress
These horsemen, doubtless, are of royal blood.

What a grand steed! See how he throws his head
And flings the foam and champs upon his bit!
But what a rider! It must be Prince John —
Or else the devil, and, as I have heard,
The difference is slight. He then, the next,
Must be Prince Charles — and both look black enough.
Where have I heard, or how, that Eric's fate
Hangs on their will? They are not his own blood,
They had a different mother, and they hate
The very earth he treads — but he, he comes
As if he trode on them! What wonder then
That these good people are so thrilled with doom,
As though the flying shuttles of the fates
Wove us all in, and shot us back and forth
With swiftly darting fibres of dismay!
  I have been hence for years, a wanderer;
Home have I none — my wits must bring me bread.
I find the children men and women now:
But though I come from going to and fro,
And voyaging up and down, my spirit feels
A sense of fatherland. This is my king!
For great Gustavus has been gathered home
And Eric takes his place and wears the crown.
This is my king! What manner of king, forsooth?
But now they halt; I must abide my time.

  The leaf that drifts upon the ocean tide
Knows nothing of the moon — nor do I know
What strange, new madness moves upon my brain
And guides me hither. Father have I none
Nor mother. I have sung so many songs
To beauty that the theme is dead and dried
Like a pressed rose; yet in my heart I hold
That faint sweet sense of loyalty and love

Which truly crowns a man.   Fool I am not
Although I toss my bauble in the air
And play with bubbles, as a painter plays,
To watch their glancing light.   The motley coat
Has its own safety and the jester's speech
Is privileged.   The fellowship of life
Is mine ; and though I stretch my very soul
That I may make a saddened pilgrim smile,.
Within me there are tears.   It is a pool·
Deep-hidden, pure, unstirred save by the wing
Of some poor thirsty bird, whose song has left
Her throat parched. up ! How little do we dream
That the true poet, wearied with the glare
And garishness of earth, steals softly in
And drinks perpetual youth at such a fount !
These contradictions, these fantastic tricks
Make up this thing of days which we call man !   ¸
Ah, now they come !

   The commonest flower that blooms
Perhaps can better understand the sun
Than the pale petals of that dainty rose
The gardener shades and tends.   Now here are those
Who soon will know if Eric is a flame
Sent forth to scathe them ; or, if, as a sun,
He shines and blesses all the realm around.
I will go talk with them.
(Exit.)

ACT I.

SCENE III.—The same.   Considerable delay in the procession.

(Enter ERIC with BURRÆUS and COUNT SVENTE STURE.)

   Bur. Have a tight rein, your majesty ! The crowd
Are clustering to welcome you.

Eric. The hornets!
I hear them buzz. I shall not let them sting!
Look there, Burræus! (Ah, you brute, be still!)
How I would gladly give this beast the spur
And charge that mass of heads! I have no doubt
They would enjoy the sport!
Bur. Your majesty
Would be so pitied, being borne away
Upon this new Bucephalus, utterly
Without control!
Eric. A leg or two perhaps,
Or else an arm, a couple of ribs, a head,
Something by which to know that I was king —
I might leave such a token here to-day
Among these peasants.

(*Shouts and cannon. Horse starts.*)

(Ha, you villainous wretch!)
Why, in the devil's name, do the people shout
And fire those guns!
(Be still, you cursed brute—
There! You were almost down!)
I never yet
Before to-day have doubted his sure foot.
Count S. Sire, on this square the noblest heads have
fallen
Under the headsman's axe: *the horse smells blood.*
Eric. Curse him and you together!

(*Drives spurs into his horse and exit.*)

Bur. (*To Count S.*) Count, that is *your* work! This is
an evil day!
Count S. And he we crown is but as the kernel dried
In the empty husk, to rattle his emptiness
In the face of the world.

Bur.   With you and me to hold,
As well as we may, this stubborn, devilish will
And curb it into patience.   Yonder, see !
He flies full gallop towards the palace gate.
I have thought to conquer him as streams are turned
By bending, not by breaking : you have been
Always the northern bear.   I went along
With the sweep of his thought to catch him as he sprang.
But you — you struck him always with the hand
When it wore the gauntlet.   Hark you, this will be
Never forgotten.   You shall bear the blame !
    Count S. Let it be so ; Amen ! Some heart must stand
Between this madman and the fatherland.
You are a scholar, doctor of the laws,
Anything, everything that learning gives :
I but a soldier, who have now and then
Shaken a grizzled chin in the battle's front.
You are a penman, and have fairly traced
Many a parchment :   I, with my sword's point,
Have left some characters not hard to read.
Keep you your course, Burræus — I keep mine !
Flatter him if you will, I shall oppose ;
And, for his father's sake, I will drive him back
From the edge of the precipice !

                    (*Exeunt.*)

ACT I.

SCENE IV. — *The square after the procession.*

(PRINCE JOHN *and* PRINCE CHARLES *enter.*)

P. John. Brother, it all goes well.   What scared the
        horse —
What could have scared the horse ? He shot along .
Like the sudden flash of a random culverin !

P. Chas. He always flashed and dashed and swore.
    If we
Are calm enough this thing may be of use.
The people liked it not. I saw them scowl;
And when a Dalecarlian miner scowls,
It wakes Gustavus Vasa in his grave.
Observe these faces; they are angry ones
And fearful ones and some are anxious-eyed,
As if disaster from the nation's heaven
Had shaken down a star.
    P. John.   Who prophesied
To Eric, that it was to be his fate
To find destruction by a fair-haired man? —
I seem long since to have heard it.
    P. Chas.   Rightly too.
It was an old crone of a witch, a hag
Without a tooth — who mumbled dreadfully
Over the rest, but made this portent plain.
She was a heathen Finn from far away,
And bade him never trust a fair-haired man —
Thou hast fair hair!
    P. John.   Enough, I see it now:
What with his superstition and his fear,
His madness and his malice, thou and I
Had little hope before: we now have less
After this burst of passion here to-day.
I trust Burræus — he will lure him on
As one might lure a goose by dropping corn!
    P. Chas. But that Count Sture! He's another man!
    P. John. Ay, that indeed. He is a man to whom
Plots are but cobwebs. You may spin your best
And calculate on every motive well;
But in steps Sture with his clumsy staff

And breaks them for you.   One can never tell
What moment he appears, —
    P. Chas.   Or what he dares
To say in court or camp.   Burræus thinks
That the Count Sture is a dangerous man
Because he is so faithful.   Here it lies
With both of us !   Settle it then at once,
Whether we seek for friendship with the Count,
Or whether we shall best secure our aim
By turning Eric's wrath upon his head.
Lightning seeks out the tall and lonely tree
Which will not bow nor hide.   I deem it best
To kindle Eric up to a thunder-storm
Which suddenly bursts and rids us of the Count.
    P. John. That is well said.   Men are not stocks and
        stones,
Pieces upon a chess-board, but living things,
With hopes and fears and passions and despairs.
And Eric is as fickle as a cloud,
As restless, and anon as full of flame
And devastation.   It is now too late
To hurt his kingship, but by watching close
The great strung harp-strings of the human soul,
Your hand or mine may play the overture
And then the devil may play the discord next !
    P. Chas. We must be going.   Stay, who is that man
There by the pillar, talking with the girl ?
That is a face I long have borne in mind —
Who can it be ?
    P. John.   Ah, now I know the man.
It is Lars Larson — jester at the court
Some years ago — no fool by any means,
Yet with a bitter, gibing tongue ; a knave,

Shrewd to his own advantage. He has much
To bind him to our use, for thou and I
Were lads so silly as to make a plea
For his old father, sentenced to be hung;
And this young stripling, aged alike with us,
Came in his gratitude and swore an oath,
Which frightened us for deadly earnestness,
That evermore he would serve thee and me.
This is the man, and, as I think, well met;
We need him and must have him.

Larson, here!

(Enter LARS.)

Lars. This is all there is left of me. I went hunting
across the Alps into Italy, and I found a rock where
Hannibal left a fire of sticks and a jug of vinegar. I
burned the rest of the sticks to warm my ten fingers,
and I have brought the vinegar home to warm my
five wits.

P. John. It is just the same fool as it was when it
went away! Come to my palace early in the morning
and I will bid my porter see that you are given entrance.

Lars. That is generally the style with great people.
'You can come when I want to see you. You can stay
until I have done with you. And then you can go hang
yourself.' I shall, however, visit your palace. But I
warn you that if you value your porter, it will be well
for you to encourage him to be prompt when I pound at
the gate. I have been known to cuff lazy porters.

(Exit.)

P. John. There is the tool, my worthy brother Charles,
That suits us better than Burræus does.
It needs a fool to beguile a crazy man.

(Exeunt.)

ACT I.

SCENE V. — *The same.*

(*Enter* LARS *and* 1ST *and* 2D WOMEN.)

1st W. What was it that he said to you, Lars?

2d W. Yes, Lars, what did he say?

Lars. He said to me that there was a new baby at his house and he wanted me to come and smile at it, so that it would n't have the colic.

1st W. You have always attempted with us those tricks that you use with the great people. But we know you too well, Master Lars. What was it he said?

Lars. Truly now, will you never tell if I tell you?

1st and 2d W. No; we will never tell.

Lars. Then, what he said to me — I guess I had better not tell you.

2d W. Tell us, Lars, or you will be worse than the old witch with her prophecy.

Lars. Well, what he said to me was that he wondered if those two handsome ladies saw King Eric's horse rush away to the palace. Because he said that it would have been curious if you had n't, for you stared at him more than all the rest of the people. And then he asked me if women always opened their eyes so wide when they stared. And I told him they did, because women have more brains than men, and their brains press their eyes almost out of their heads when they are excited. That's all, my children. Peace be with you! — as the elephant said when he tramped on the puppy-dog.

(*Exit.*)

2d W. Lars talks sense and nonsense by turns. He does not please me. But he thinks he does. King Eric now is a far handsomer man.

1st W. Wait! here is Catherine Mone. Let us hear what a handsome woman thinks of your handsome man!

(*Enter* CATHERINE.)

2d W. Well met, Catherine. We were going home.

Cath. And so was I. Has it not been a strange day? There is surely something in the air which makes me sad and fearful. And how suddenly the procession broke up and dispersed!

1st W. Ay! the nobles and the military were somehow ill at ease. And then King Eric's horse took fright and ran away. I pray that the king be not hurt. We watched him, however, and he seemed to sit in his saddle safely.

2d W. Was he not fine, Catherine? Had he not a grave face, with that pointed beard and that heavy thatching to his lip, so that one could scarcely see his white teeth. And then he smiled and laughed — and then the cannons fired and away rushed the horse! Oh, it was frightful!

Cath. Yes; I saw it all. It was a noble picture. He is a king, indeed.

2d W. You say but little. You do not remember his splendid diamonds and his white silk suit; his great black hat with its ostrich feather; his red boots, his golden spurs, his cloak!

Cath. I remember all these, but it was the face of which I was thinking. Farewell!

(*Exeunt.*)

ACT II.

SCENE I. — *A room in the palace.*

(*Enter* ERIC, BURRÆUS, LARS *and* COUNT STURE.)

Eric. Burræus, thou art doctor; write a scroll

In the best of art and send it to Lorraine.
Say to the Princess Renee that I hope
My suit may be acceptable. As I hear
She is a woman well-apportioned, fair
And worthy of our throne in Sweden. Haste,
And frame the document!

(*Exit* BURRÆUS.)

Lars.   Your majesty!
I beg that if you get her and do n't want her, you would
kindly remember a poor fool who has not your wit to
use fine expressions. Perhaps the Princess Renee, of
Lorraine, might help me to· dignify myself in a proper
manner.

Eric. Ha! ha! Thou art a merry fool indeed,
And so John said — I think you came from John? —
But I would have you·altogether forget
That you have ever known a lord but me.
Yet, after all, and when all else is said,
I do confess that jests are often dull.
They batter feebly on a weary brain ;
Like birds against a lighted casement's rim,
They fly the darkness and they seek the light,
And between light and darkness there they fall
And die in stupidness.

                    Count, I know I seem
A·different man at times, and now and then
I have, I do believe, a better self.

Count S. (*With emotion.*) Alas, my·lord, it is a fatal truth!
I well remember times and seasons marked
By any other mood than this, which now
Seems like a bivouac before a fight —
All stilled, with hope of victory beyond.
I fear me, sire, that when I best would aid

You, as against yourself, you do forget
That I would serve you even to the death.

Eric. Believe me, my good Sture, I do not
Forsake my father's friends.   My books all warn
Against such conduct.   Evil future comes
From this more than all else.   If I were now
A Romanist, a follower of the Pope,
I would tell over on my breviary
The pithiest prayers to ward off such a speech.

Lars. Oh, that's easily done !   You can make a small
fire of incense and gently burn up a whole prayer book.
Rises to heaven in sweet odors.like Master Tetzel's par-
doned souls.   For my part, I prefer beer and pudding to
holy water and penance.   These quiet my conscience
better than an ill-digested breviary.   That makes me
think of a row of holy candles.   Light them for the
angels to look upon, and presently out they go with a bad
smell.   Nay, nay, cousin, work while you pray, and be
ready to catch another princess if the Princess Renee
should take flight.

Eric. True, my good fool !   Another princess now
Would prove a wise direction for the mind.
Besides, your own heart centres on Lorraine,
And I must save you from your melancholy.
Who is there next?   Come, name her !

Lars. There's the Scottish queen, Mary — a paragon
of beauty ; the gentlemen hold their hats over their
faces and peer through pin holes to look at her.   She is
blindingly beautiful.   Her gardener invites her to help
him with his crooked trees.   She smiles at the tree and,
presto ! it bends toward her and all is well.   'Twere as
easy for such a woman to make the world wag worthily,
as for me to toss my bauble !

Eric. That is high praise : she shall be notified
Of our approval.   Call me in that scribe
And bid him hasten to Burræus with it!
   Count S. Stay! Not so soon, your majesty! There lives
In England one Elizabeth, a queen
Far beyond Mary, both in state and wit.
Try her and be in earnest; such a thought
Might well beseem Gustavus Vasa's son.
To add to Sweden England, with her arms,
Her fleets, her nobles and her learned men,
'Twould be as though, across the bridge Bifrost,
The hosts of ancient heroes came again;
As if Valhalla opened wide her doors
And the great mead-horns were uplifted high
And the long ships sprang flashing o'er the brine!
Son of Gustavus Vasa, seek that queen!
   Eric. It shall be done.   Go! call another scribe.
   Count S. (*Aside.*) Now do I think that the last hope
     is gone!
He leaps up like a flame before the breath;
Or like a butterfly, from flower to flower,
The wind blows him along!
                    O empty, empty,
And worse than empty! Flattered by a fool,
Tricked by a scholar, duped by wily John,
And I, the only friend, left powerless!
I tried him with Elizabeth and now
The Prince of Hesse soon will find it out
And Princess Catherine, the only hope
With a thread to hold it, will be rent away,
And all the world will laugh and mock and jeer!
              (*Exit.*)
   Eric. (*To Lars.*) I have a name for thee, good fool, a name

Which may befit thee.   Hearken ! This it is :
"Hercules Cæsar Anthony Steinberg."
Henceforth be reckoned my prime minister.
Away with this Burræus — he's an ass !
Away with this Count Sture — he's a fool,
A solemn idiot muttering in his sleeve ! —
Thou art the wise man only of the three.
For see ! This bald Burræus bends and fawns,
And this Count Sture scowls and thwarts my will,
And the Prince John — how I do hate Prince John ! —
Lays traps in which to catch me.

                    Better a fool,
With a nimble tongue and store of merry songs,
Than these who only think they have more brains.
Come, fool, and sing until I fall asleep !

   Lars. (*Sings.*)

> *Over the sea, over the sea !*
> *The little bird sang in the mulberry tree ;*
> *And she said ' These berries are sweet to me,'*
> *Up in the top of the mulberry tree.*
>
> *Over the sea, over the sea !*
> *The gray worm crawled in the mulberry tree ;*
> *And she said, ' These leaves are the leaves for me,*
> *Up in the top of the mulberry tree.*
>
> *Over the sea, over the sea !*
> *The Chinaman came to the mulberry tree ;*
> *And he said, ' This silk has been spun for me,'*
> *Up in the top of the mulberry tree.*
>
> *Over the sea, over the sea !*
> *Away with your bird in the mulberry tree ;*
> *And hail to the worm who spins so free,*
> *Up in the top of the mulberry tree !*

(*Aside.*)
Gone to sleep without his allegory ! Well, that is like

the world in general. Lars Larson, you are now Hercules Cæsar Anthony Steinberg. There may be a time hereafter when you can come out of your slough as a man. Meanwhile, spin your silk, you gray worm!

(*Exit.*)

ACT II.

SCENE II. — *A room in Prince John's palace.*

(*Enter* PRINCE JOHN *and* PRINCE CHARLES.)

P. John. The latest messages that reach to me
Show that our Lars has been the very front
And soul of all these doings at the court.
He pulls the strings and then the puppets dance!
He is the titled fool; he has a name
Which some declare is Eric's special gift;
He wears a fool's cap half a fathom long
Which jingles as he goes, and bells enough
To make a perfect Aaron, fringe his robe.
Such a high priest of folly, I could swear,
Was never known before.
   P. Chas.   Is it not time
That we had gathered in *our* puppet's wires
And pulled them as we please?
   P. John.   That was our plan
When he was put where Eric could perceive
His strange and wild attractions. He is there,
Close in his confidence. No one suspects
That any slightest thread runs thence to us;
For it was so contrived, that he fled from me
With stories of ill-usage, fear and pain,
To Eric. Therefore, Eric took him in
That he might anger me. Ha! ha! it was

So well arranged that even Count Sture thinks
The fool is trusty — yet he is no fool,
As you shall see.   He comes to us anon.
Step you behind the arras.   He will drop
The fool's tone and will meet me as a man.

(*Exit* CHARLES.   *Enter a* SERVANT.)

Serv. My lord, one waits to speak with you.
P. John. Bring him within !

(*Exit* SERVANT.   *Enter* LARS, *disguised.*)

Well, sir, what wish you ?
Lars. Only to ask you how you like your fool.
P. John. Fellow, thou hast deceived me spite of all.
Lars. What wonder, when I masquerade all day,
That sometimes I should choose to be a man —
And yet I keep the edge upon my tongue
Like any fool.   Forgive me then, my lord,
That I may change my court but not my soul.
P. John. Thou art forgiven.   Listen now and note
What I shall say.   The day was when the king
Drew forth thy father from a shameful death,
And thou did'st come, a little lad, to me,
Scarce older than thyself, with vows and tears
Of gratitude and service, for I think
I somewhat moved my father to spare thine.
The years have passed, but thou dost not forget
These things, Lars Larson ?
Lars.   Nay, my lord, not I.
P. John. What I expect of thee is merely this :
My brother holds a causeless prejudice,
A superstition even, against myself.
Thou hast his ear and, some men say, his heart.
Bend thou his heart and let me see it bend,

So that my father's son may speedily,
Before this land, be near his brother's side.

Lars. That is, my lord, go in and out at court
As does Count Svente Sture?

P. John.   So I mean.
That is sufficient for thy duty now.
Use this to brighten up thy wit with wine,
                    (*Gives him a purse.*)
And let the broad gold pieces smile at thee
And pave thy way to many pieces more.

Lars. I thank your highness!

                    (*Exit.   Re-enter* CHARLES.)

P. John. There then, good brother Charles, appears a
        way
Opening into the palace.   Once within,
'Tis a poor spider cannot keep the web
He takes without construction.

P. Chas.   Surely, John;
But fools are edge-tools, ever sharp and keen,
Yet hardly to be trusted.   Do you trust him?

P. John. With nothing but the task I set for him.
It doth not fit a high estate to wind
And turn and burrow dirtily for itself.
One sends the weasel in to hunt the rat
And stays without and waits.   Avoid thou, then,
The possible complications which result
Where the commander plays the pioneer
And saps and mines with calloused, common hands.
Do thou sit far aloof—then if thy plot
Be smitten in its progress, let it fall
And crush the lesser plotter — thou art safe!
I trust no human soul, unless it be
Bound life and death, as thou art, in the mesh

In which I am. There is a bond, indeed,
Of hate which binds men firmer than in love.
We hate that Eric, brother, do we not?

P. Chas. Assuredly, and he in turn hates us,
And the fool ministers between. What next
May happen if upon the fool's false wit
We make an ice bridge and essay to pass,
But in mid-stream the treacherous, fatal thing
Cracks to the current of a maddened brain,
And we be swept away as well as he?

P. John. He, then, were best adrift in the Skager Rack,
On an ice-floe in the summer. Hell is hot,
And even a fool may melt into the gulf.—
But fear me not; my patience is like death.

(Exeunt.)

ACT. II.

SCENE III. — *In the palace at Stockholm.*

(*Enter* ERIC *and* BURRÆUS.)

Eric. Master Burræus, many a time have I
Advised that you should earnestly press that suit
To the Princess of Lorraine. I also gave
Direction for a proper document
To Scotland's Mary. If the fool speak true,
She is the fairest of the beautiful.
He called her such a star as shines by night,
When air is still and earth is hushed in sleep,
On some calm fiord. Through the rifted walls
The rays fall, and they sink into the soul
Of the pure lake that lies below the star,
And star and lake together blend in one;
And then there comes a breath and, as it stirs

The depths beneath and the star trembles too,
The loftier heaven untremblingly looks down,
And the high soul and the deep soul are one;
And the man's queen is also queen of men.

Bur. Was that, then, what the fool said? If I thought
He conjured up such fancies, I should think
A thousand other things!

    Eric.   What other things?

    Bur. Nothing but this, your majesty: that fools
Are seldom given to lofty sentiment.

    Eric. But he is, and I think the less of you,
With your Greek and Latin and outlandish tongues,
Because you sneer.

              Burræus, I must make
This kingdom smaller by my brother John.

    Bur. Indeed? Why so?

    Eric.   He is a fair-haired man,
And a fair-haired man is fated, so I learn,
To be my ruin.

          Draw the warrant out!
Take him for treason!

    Bur.   But, your majesty —

    Eric. Another moment and I add you too,
And, if you let him escape, I add you still!

           '(*Exit* BURRÆUS.)

Yes, he's a traitor; all of them are traitors.
They whisper and they point; they plot, they scheme;
I verily believe there is not one
Whom I can trust. Ho, there! send in my fool;
Send Hercules Cæsar!

        (*Enter* LARS.)

Sing to me, fool; the devil, as I hear,
Makes himself tunes with fetter-locks and chains,

And when the angels hover round and strike
Their small, sweet harps of gold, he stops his ears
And dives to the bottomless pit.

Strike up, I say !

Lars. (*Sings.*)

> *Heigh-ho, heigh-ho !*
> *The lark sprang up,*
> *And she shook the dew from the buttercup,*
> *Over the world below.*
>
> *Heigh-ho, heigh-ho !*
> *The lark soared high,*
> *And she caught the glory out of the sky,*
> *Over the world below.*
>
> *Heigh-ho, heigh-ho !*
> *Spring up, my heart !*
> *For the day has come and the shades depart,*
> *Over the world below.*

Eric. Leave me, for I would have a little rest.
Thy song is like a pillow of the turf,
From which I look up deep within the sky.

(Exit Lars.)

My God, what does it mean ! I loathe myself,
I hate all men, but not less than I fear
Them and myself. John now is cast in chains —
Would he were dead !

I wonder, am I mad ?

One moment poetry, the next a prayer,
The next a curse. It is like Saul, the king
Of whom the Lutherans read. I saw a bird
With a broken wing ; it tried to fly, but still
It beat about in circles, dashed itself
Down on the ground and cried in shrill, short screams.
It was so crazed by fear, so impotent

In effort — and one came and set his foot
Upon its neck and crushed it.

     So am I
A bird with broken wing. Only this fool
Can touch my sadness. That Burræus now
Is a dull pedant. Sture angers me
With pestilent appeals and much advice.
John is in prison; thank the Lord for that !
Curses on Charles; his time is coming soon !
Or is it mine that comes ?

     Will the fair-haired man
Set foot upon *my* throat ?

     I will go now
And write these words. They are a prophecy.
I'll write them — and amend.

     But John — but John ?
No; John must stay in prison. Time enough
To think of that to-morrow. Danger lurks
In the tread of John.

     The fool, at least, is safe ;
But Sture is a treacherous enemy !

    (*Exit.*)

ACT II.

SCENE IV. — *The council chamber.*

(BURRÆUS *seated at his desk.*)

Bur. Aha ! it is a thing to be observed
That frequently, in talking with ourselves,
Words slip out here and there. No lips so tight
Were ever made, that nothing could leak through.
And when our royal master sinks to sleep,
He mutters and he groans, he starts and cries,

So that the pages in the ante-chamber
Can overhear him.
                                    I could set John free,
But that I fear it would be little use.
I know that Goran Persson far too well
To fancy he would leave the king uninstigated
Against myself. He is a jealous man —
Jealous of me, most jealous of the Count.
This palace fills with plots. Each day goes forth
An mbassy for some new princess' hand,
And the state treasury fails. The taxes run
Like a summer torrent fed by the avalanche.
The _nore I am persuasive, still the more
He grows abusive, truculent and fierce.
Save thyself then, Burræus, and bring forth
John to the kingdom, for if John the duke
Be John the king, thou art his counselor.
And now, because these tangled threads will twine
Inevitably closer, here it seems
Comes Goran Persson.

(*Enter* PERSSON.)

Per. Hail and good cheer, Burræus! How goes on
That commentary of thine?
    Bur.   Oh, constantly
As one can press it, when forever called
Up to the surface to be Cupid's clerk.
    Per. And what is latest?
    Bur.   This! another scroll
Forsooth, to the Virgin Queen.
    Per. What says it then?
    Bur.   It bids her to take note
That Eric presently will come to woo,
And bring his troops behind him.

Per.   What return
Had the last embassy ?

Bur.   She sent reply,
That as she liked the messenger so ill,
The message so much worse, it would be strange
If she should like the master.

Per.   And he said ? —

Bur. He said that he, himself, should go straightway ;
And bade me draft another protocol !

Per. And thou hast done it ! Why, most worthy sage,
We soon shall have thee blooming as the May ;
And Eric shall be married, much to the ease
Of certain troubled brains, like thine and mine.
Where is the king then, this auspicious hour ?
Listens he to the music of his fool —
A marvelous sweet singer, by the way —
Or is he thinking of Duke John, perchance?

Bur. He is among his books.

(Exit PERSSON.)

Yes ; go thy way
And find him, to pour poison in his ear.

(Exit.)

ACT II.

SCENE V. — The library.

(Enter PERSSON, to ERIC who is reading, while LARS is
stretched on a rug.</i>)</div>

Per. Your majesty is occupied to-day ?
I would not trouble your attention now ;
Permit me to depart.

Eric.   Persson, remain !
I have a question I would put to you.

Nay, never mind the fool; he basks in the sun
And catches dancing motes.

      By Odin, now
That is a picture! See, he lies on the rug
Of tiger skin, broad on his back, the sun
Streaming across his spangles, knee upreared
And leg on knee, and ankle held in hand.
Ho! motley fool, what dost thou think about?

 Lars. (Sings.)

> *I'm thinking, I'm thinking*
> *All the summer day,*
> *I'm thinking of a little bird*
> *That flew so far away.*
>
> *So far away, so far away,*
> *So far away she flew,*
> *I'm thinking what a tiny speck*
> *Has melted in the blue.*
>
> *A little bird, a little bird,*
> *She took my heart along,*
> *She took my heart so far away,*
> *And only left a song.*

 Per. Right well sung, Hercules. I wonder now
If in this mode we wear the lion's skin
Instead of the spotted tiger's.

 Lars. (On his back.) You shall have this
To clothe yourself withal. I like not cats.
They purr too much for things with teeth and claws,
That crouch and watch and spring—

 Eric.   Peace then, thou fool!
And let this counselor chatter in mine ear.
Proceed, most learned master!

 Per.   May I know
If Duke John is in prison?

Eric.   Ay, indeed,
Duke John *is* fast in prison.

                    There he stays
In comfort, with old waters in a jug
And daily manna, furnished by the loaf.

   Per. How long shall he be there?

   Eric.   How long? Until
He bites his finger nails into the quick,
Until he knows the spiders and the rats,
And every individual, separate stone
That forms his cell — until he leaves his hope
Buried beneath a slab, with a shackle bolt
Over its heart.

   Per.   My noble, excellent lord,
It is most wisely, temperately said,
For I have reason to imagine now,
That John, let loose, is such a beast of prey
As though that tiger came and took his skin,
And ramped and raged among us. Wisdom says,
Strong bars and solid chains become a beast.—
Some beasts I like not living.

            (LARS *starts.*)

                    See the fool!
Why, man, the tiger skin is not alive.

   Lars. (*Peevishly.*) Well, if it is n't alive, it has fleas in it and one-bit me.

   Eric. What would you then, Persson?

   Per.   Most gracious king,
It is expedient always that we take
The bear when we find his den.

   Eric.   Some hunters fear
To enter single-handed to the fight.

   Per. 'Tis easy to besiege him.

Eric.   Meanest thou
To fasten up the entrance to the cave
And let the bear starve on !
  Per.   Assuredly.
The heavens shut up their bread if angels cease
To drop the manna on us by the loaf ;
And now and then a fountain may run dry
Without your fault or mine.   Judicious kings
Ticket and label such unpleasant folk,
And leave them to themselves.   I would not say
Do any violence, shed any blood ;
Only, forget him, quietly ignore
The fact that he exists.
  Eric.   Enough, go see
These orders under signet.   Take my ring.
Say to the jailor what you said to me.—
Well, fool, what now ?

  Lars. Oh, nothing, only I read once in Solomon that
a live dog was better than a dead lion — or a dead tiger,
either, I suppose.   Cousin, what fun it will be to hold
John up and let him bark by-and-by.   The wind-pipe,
brethren, is, as it were, a flute, but you cannot play on it
if the breath be gone.   Mayhap we shall need John to
extol our clemency ere all is over.

  Per. This is a fool's counsel, sire.   Never think
That John deserves reprieve.   His teeth are sharp,
His claws are long, his heart is filled with hate.

  Eric. But bars are strong.   I trust a prison grate.
Give back my ring.   Let the fool have his way.

  Per. Your majesty is ever kind and good ;
Too kind and good for your own interests.

(Exeunt.)

ACT III.

(*Enter* ERIC *and* COUNT STURE *in carriage. A group of women, &c., at a distance.*)

Eric. What is that crowd? Where are my guards?
　　Come, sir,
Draw up those horses!
　　　　　　　　Go, Count Sture; see
What this may mean, for it seems peaceable.

　　　　　　　(*Exit* STURE.)

Drive nearer, coachman!

　　　　　　　(*Re-enter* STURE.)

　　　　　　　　Well, what is it, then?
Count S. Your majesty, some clumsy wagon wheel
Has struck and harmed a pretty peasant girl,
A seller of flowers. The people cluster round,
And that is all — there is no danger here.
It might be well, perchance, if you would show
A moment's notice; subjects love to feel
Their king forgets them not.
　Eric. 　　　　　' She's pretty, eh?
It is not a bad notion to be kind,
Especially when one can have the chance
Without an insurrection.
　　　　　　　Let me out!

(*Draws near to* CATHERINE MONE, *who lies on the pavement, supported by women.*)

　1*st W.* Poor dear! poor dear! she hardly breathes at
　　all.
　2*d W.* Yes, her heart beats; stand back and give her
　　air.

Eric. Good people, what is this?

2d W. An accident.

1st W. She is much hurt; she has not yet come to.

Eric. Lift her head higher — there! Is a surgeon near
Who may be had?

Be quick and fetch him then.

(*As* ERIC *bends over her,* CATHERINE *opens her eyes.*)

Cath. The king!

People. God bless your majesty!

Eric. Yes; I am he!
Bear this poor child to the palace; she shall be
Nursed by my sister and her waiting maids.
Stay with them, Count, and care that this be done.

(*Enters carriage. Exeunt people and* COUNT STURE
attending CATHERINE.)

What eyes! I never saw such eyes before.
They may be gray or blue or brown or violet,
But they shot into my soul!

And what a calm
Shone in their light! It was like the lofty star
In the clear lake, of which the jester sings.
I must see more of them. · I *will* see more.
I want those eyes to have them for my own!
Music is rest, but love is hope and peace.

(*Exit.*)

ACT III.

SCENE II. — *The evening of the same day. The palace at
Stockholm.*

(*Enter* ERIC, COUNT STURE, LARS *and* ATTENDANTS.)

Count S. The maiden, sire, is safely placed and well.

A trifle shaken, but no further hurt
Than a blue bruise on her temple.

                      If I thought
That you would care, I might recall her name
And parentage.

    Eric.   Why should you pause at that?
Proceed and tell me!

    Count S.   She is Catherine Mone,
Granddaughter of a veteran who fought
Under the great Gustavus. Him I saw
In many a battle, always true as steel.
Subordinate in station, but in soul
Superior to generals of the line.
And of herself, I dare to say but this,
As a rough soldier, that the flowers she sells
Are like her spirit, ever fresh and pure.
She has a thoughtful mind; she loves and learns
As I could wish a daughter of my own
To love and learn.

    Eric.   Go, bid her come to me.
I would speak with her and without delay.

             (*Exit* STURE.)

Call to me Hercules Cæsar! Let him sing.

    (LARS *advances from among the* ATTENDANTS.)

    Lars. The matter with me is that my music box is full
of green fields and birds and blue sky, so I went down
by the shore of the sea after a new pattern and there I
got a song. That is the way to get songs! "Open your
mouth," says the clam, "and let the tide flow in." But
these gentlemen here yawn immensely and capture nothing, unless it be an unseasonable fly or a suicidal gnat.
Hither to me, seventeen of you! Twist me up this tenor

string. Oh, that I had Master Rabelais here to waken your wits, so you might appreciate my song!

(*Several* ATTENDANTS *surround* LARS, *laughing and pushing each other.*)

Leave alone, you villains! Your huge fists do me no good! See here, masters. With this small key I shall tune my string and you may go caper. That will be fine practice for a dance at the end of a rope. "Listen now, with all your ears," as the donkeys said when they heard the nightingale!

(*Sings.*)

On the white sea sand,
By the side of the land,
* I wandered and sang,*
With my harp in my hand.

I sang of the sea
With its mystery,
* Of the ships which pass*
Unmindful of me.

But a bird drew near,
A bird so dear,
* White-winged and fearless,*
And sang in my ear :

" O singer, wait
For thy coming fate,
* Which riseth to meet thee*
With sails elate !

" From hope's eclipse,
From voiceless lips,
* There is sent thee one*
Of love's sweet ships.

" Already the light
Of a morning bright, ·
At the rim of the world,
Shows a sail so white ! "

And now will I stand,
With my harp in my hand,
And sing to my ship,
Till she comes to land !

Eric. Leave me, ye rascals ! Let the Count come in
And bring the girl.

(*Exeunt.*)

Ah, here, at length, he comes.

(*Enter* Count *and* Catherine.)

Count S. This is the maiden, sire, of whom we spoke.
Eric. Your name, what is it ?
Cath.   Catherine, my lord.
Eric. Your father ?
Cath.   He is now a soldier, sire.
Eric. Your mother ?
Cath.   She, alas, long since is dead.
Eric. Tell me, then, of yourself —

(*Aside.*)

Those eyes ! those eyes !
Cath. What should I tell ? Your majesty, the brook
That ripples down the hill sings on and on,
The same monotonous strain. And thus my life
Has murmured like a brook, always the same.
Eric. I care not. I would hear of that same brook,
From spring to valley — it will rest my ear.
Cath. I am a peasant girl, your majesty.
My father's father was a soldier too,
A good and wise old man. He used to call

Me to his side and tell me simple tales
Of holy men.   And I would sit and hear
How huge Goliath bowed before the stone
Which David slung — how Samson went away
With the broad gates of Gaza on his back —
How the tall pillar brightened o'er the plain
And the white manna, dropping through its light,
Descended like the snow, when, on the hills,
The red-beard Thor flings his swift lances up.
These tales and many more, but most of all,
How the White Christ, that splendid, holy form,
Walked on the stormy and unfrozen sea,
Which tossed Him high and sank Him low, but still
By crag or valley bore Him to His own.
And then, in summer, I must feed the cows,
Or gather berries, or, in nooks and dells
Of the dark mountains, pick the fairest flowers
That nestle nearest to the rocky heart.

   Your majesty, perchance, has never seen
A spring in the midst of moss.   On either hand
The alders and the willows shade it well.
The birds come there to drink and raise their hearts
In praise, and sing a song and fly away.
There the green moss is fresh as emerald,
With little peering, ruddy, goblin-eyes.
And there the insects of the summer hours
Sport in the long, long day — the dragon-fly
Hangs motionless, with wings which move so swift
As to elude the sight.   And then, if one
Stirs the fine pool and muddies all its stream,
The rising crystal will not suffer that,
But steadily and constantly it bursts
Out of the soul of nature and redeems

The lovely waters from a trace of stain.
This was my life : I only know it now
Because I bear sweet flowers about the street,
And every one is good to me, and some
Are better than the rest. No trouble comes
But tears can wash it from me.

May I go ?

Eric. Catherine, remain! Thou art henceforth to be
A maid of honor at my sister's call.
Thy father shall be cared for — there is none
But only thou it seems — but only thou.
And now depart.

(*Exit* CATHERINE.)

ACT III

SCENE III. — *The palace at Stockholm.*

(ERIC *alone.*)

Eric. Calmness and peace at last ! God send it speed
To roll and rise as in some mighty sea,
Which buries towers and palaces and spreads
A smooth, unrippled surface to the star !
For she is such a star.

Send Sture here !

(*Enter* STURE.)

Count S. What would your majesty ?
Eric. Only this, my Count,
That now, at length, I feel upon my soul
The covering wings of peace. The eider-down
Is not more soft and warm ; my heart is full ;
I could most heartily go hence to heaven.

Count S. Most gracious lord, sincerely do I pray,
That thus we reach the end of a weary road !

Eric. Weep not, good Sture; rather smile again,
For the great kingdom shall go on apace,
When in the circling systems of my soul
The central sun of purpose takes his throne.

(*Enter* LARS.)

Lars. I am somewhat downcast, master o' mine, and I
have come to get consolation. Will you hear a song?
A girl winked at me out of a window and I made the
song on the spot, spinning my cap by its tassel and giv-
ing my dog a kick between the stanzas. And even then
she didn't understand my melancholy, so I have come
to you with it.

(*Sings.*)

My love has eyes so blue,
My love has eyes so true ;
   They are eyes that are old as the sky is old,
And yet they are ever new !

My love has eyes so kind,
She sees that love is blind ;
   For the blindest love is the deepest love
That ever the soul can find.

My love has eyes that shine
With light and hope divine ;
   And I love their light, for I have no light
Till the eyes of my love are mine.

(*Enter* BURRÆUS.)

Bur. What now? more music! Always singing songs!
You spin them easily, Master Hercules,
As with Omphale's distaff.

Eric.   Peace, I say!
And get you to your places, all of you —
All, save Burræus.

       Doctor, come with me
Into the tower that we may see the stars.
 Bur. I can but tell you the old story still.
Fixed in their courses move the selfsame spheres,
And I, your majesty, may say no more
Nor less than there is written. Urge me not
To try anew the purpose of the stars;
For if those holy chariot wheels should move
Adverse to man, they track across his heart
Unwonted sorrows.
 Eric.   Nonsense! Heaven and earth
Lie cradled in eternity's great hand,
Which rocks them softly to oblivion.
And think'st thou, then, that in those spaces high
Thy fate or mine should tremble in the grasp
Which holds large interests? Nay! Love is lord
Of heaven and earth, and, if he say the word,
No star shall bend an unpropitious ray,
No baleful fire shall light my earthly way.
 Bur. Be it then as you will. But, sire, beware
To tempt too often that mysterious house
Wherein I see strange and disjointed things,
Which writhe like broken serpents. If I put
Piece unto piece, I can discern a woe
To happen — how, I know not — but 't is there.
 Eric. Peace reigns on earth — 't is peace among the
  stars.
I have no fear; climb up and question them!
Thrust thy sharp query in the face of fate,
And fate will follow to the stronger will.
 Bur. You are not always thus, my lord.
 Eric.   I know
That I am often gloomy and oppressed

With apprehension. Here I cast it off.
My soul is taught more wisely now than then.
Speak with the stars, and if they scowl at me,
So much the worse for them !
  Bur.   I trust, indeed,
That they may prove most gracious.
  Eric.   Nay, they *shall*
Or I will practice with the lenses too
And read them for myself.

      (*Exeunt.*)

ACT III.

SCENE IV. — *A town.*

(*Enter* BURRÆUS *and* ERIC.)

Bur. Once more then, sire, I cast your horoscope.
Once more I plot and designate the place
That he, your reigning planet, shall assume
In passing through the houses of the night.
Venus, the star of love, is rising now ;
And in conjunction, in the seventh house,
With Jupiter, I see a marriage marked
Most fortunately. But Mars, the lord of war,
Appears in the eighth house, the house of death.
Your majesty, however, may take hope,
Since in the eleventh house — the house of friends —
I find devoted love and faithful hearts.
  Eric. What of the fair-haired man ?
  Bur.   He is not there.
He disappears ; I know not anything
About him further.
  Eric.   What then of the house
In which that marriage stands ?

Bur. I said to you it would be fortunate.
And yet, in the twelfth house, captivity
Is dimly shadowed, and the second house
Displays the loss of wealth.
    Eric.   Did you not say
That the third house was brethren, and the fourth,
Relations ? What of them ?
    Bur.   Nothing I see
To cause anxiety. The marriage house,
Again I say, is fortunate.
    Eric.   Good cheer !
Thou shalt be honored and repaid for this.
And yet how strange, how very strange it is,
That stars which shine unalterably far off,
(If half that is said be true,) should keep an eye,
An ever watchful eye, on thee and me,
And rule our destinies as they circle round
The world in which we live.
                    Descend, dear sir,
To the common level of the sleeping folk.
I, for one moment, will observe the star
That rises now and shines against the east.
What is its name ? Ah, Venus !
                      Well, go down.
        (Exeunt.)

ACT IV.

SCENE I. — *A room in the palace.*

Cath. And I am here — and here I am indeed.
It is and yet is not a prison house.
They teach the bird to sing when she is caged,
For so they make her listen and obey,

And so they make me listen in my cage.
My friends disown me in the vilest terms
That can be fashioned at the devil's forge,
And used for arrows against my poor heart.
Yet I am free from blame. None is more kind
Than the very king they sneer at constantly.

(*A knock.*)

Who knocks? Come in!

                        Great heavens, is it you,
Sten Leyonhufwud? Your life is not safe!

  Sten. Oh, Catherine, I must see you if I die!
Do you remember that we are betrothed,
That I have lived in hope of having you —
That even now I have escaped the guard
To see you here, and plead once more with you
To leave this gilded infamy?

  Cath.   Hear me, Sten.
Why should you come, if you could think me base
And bad enough to dwell in such a place?

  Sten. I care not, Catherine, what you may be,
By what name people call you. I alone
Will hold and shield you all the closer for it.
Leave this bad king, for love's sake and for God's,
If not for mine, and come away with me.

  Cath. Sten Leyonhufwud, you have done me wrong —
Wrong of the blackest that a man can do.
You offer love and insult in a breath.

  Sten. Only an instant, Catherine. Hear me, still!
The city rings with it — the people say
A thousand devilish things — your name is blown
Like thistle-down and wheresoe'er it lights
A spiny thistle springs and falls to seed,
And so the story spreads.

                              I dare all this
Because I love you.   Never heed the shame,
For I will be between its hurt and you.

    Cath. This is enough, Sten Leyonhufwud!   So
You cannot think me, even as I am,
Pure and above reproach?   Nay, no more words.
Evade the guard and get thee hence.   Away !

    Sten. I knew it was so — I felt it.   False and foul,
Farewell !

        (*Rushes out.   Enter* GORAN PERSSON.)

    Per. Who left this room an instant since ?
    Cath. It was a sergeant, sir, one of the guard.
    Per. What was he doing here ?
    Cath.   I cannot tell.
    Per. You cannot, or you will not ?
    Cath.   Cannot, sir.
    Per. This matter, woman, shall most surely reach
The ears of the king. ¡

        (*Exeunt.*)

ACT IV.

SCENE II. — *A room in the palace.*

(ERIC *seated.   Enter* PERSSON.)

    Per. It is, perhaps, well worth your thought, my lord,
That some flower girls permit a bee or two ;
And bees steal honey, mark you.
    Eric.   What — what — what !
    Per. Oh, it is nothing — everybody knows.
    Eric. Knows what ?
    Per. The general principles of flower girls.
Boquets they are, tied up — a mass of color

Held by a string, and if the string should break,
That is the end.

Eric. What do you mean, you hound!

Per. That then the stalks and flowers are in the dirt,
And no one ever cares to pick them up.

Eric. A thousand devils! Is it Catherine?

Per. What Catherine? There is a waiting maid
To your sister, once a flower girl — her I mean.

Eric. What of her? Speak!

Per. Only a lover, sire.

Eric. *Only* a lover! I will have his head!
Fire and death and fury! Find him out!

(*Exit* PERSSON *and enter* STURE.)

Count S. My lord, your brother?

Eric. What about my brother?

Count S. He lies in the dungeon now for many weeks.
His life runs low; he is your father's son —
Son of Gustavus Vasa, like yourself.

Eric. And if he were ten thousand times the son
Of fifty thousand Vasas, he should die.

Count S. Nay, nay, your majesty! You cannot mean
To give Prince John an ignominious death?

Eric. By Odin, yes! He burrows, plots and schemes,
Even in his dungeon. Oh, I could go down
And take him by the throat and strangle him,
And beat his villainous head against the wall.

Count S. For God's sake, pause!

Eric. I will not have a word
Of impudent interference!

Oh, you think
You have gray hairs, and gray hairs should be safe.
Look to it then, and ask no help for John.
Here, take this signet! Have him instantly

Brought forth to death !

Count S.   Heaven help him and you !

Eric. Depart at once and do as I have bid !

Count S. I was your father's friend ; I am your friend ;
A better friend to you than you can be
To yourself —

Eric.   Then out of my sight at once,
And put that scoundrel's head under the ax !

Count S. This is outrageous.   Calm yourself; you
     rave.

Eric. Not more than you, you traitor ! Ah, I know
All your dark plots.   You try to set John free,
And then to murder me that he may rule.

Count S. By the great God, it is an infamous lie !

Eric. Lie ! lie ! and to your king !

            (*Draws his sword.*)

                      Down with you !

Count S. (*Folding his arms.*) Strike ! I shall be well
     rid of all the pain !

     (*Eric thrusts him through.   He falls and dies.*)

ACT IV.

SCENE III. — *The study of Burræus.*

(*To him enter* PERSSON *and a* GUARD OF SOLDIERS.)

Per. Come, master Doctor ! Come ! Away to jail !

Bur. Why should I come ?

Per.   Here is the warrant.   Here
Are reasons plenty.   Gather up your cloak
And come along.

Bur.   Never !

Per.   Oh, yes, you will !

Advance, my men! Take care; he has a sword.—
Now will you come?

    Bur.   Never, I say!

    Per.   Draw near!
Lunge at him! That's the way! One at a time!
Come, now! Will you go?

    Bur.   Never! God help me!

    Per. So lunge away, my men! We cannot wait.
Dead or alive we want him. Perhaps dead
He makes the least disturbance. Take a pike;
It reaches further than a sword, you know.
Pin him against the wall!—

                      There, that is right.

    Bur. (*Gasping.*) Traitor—and villain—doom—will
    come—to you.

                (*Dies. Exeunt.*)

ACT IV.

SCENE IV. — *A by-street in Stockholm.*

(*Enter the three* WOMEN.)

1st W. This news is dreadful. I can scarce believe it.

3d W. Did I not tell you he was a child of sorrow to
the land?

2d W. And they say that Lars is the court jester, and
that he is the one they call Hercules Cæsar, who rides
backward on the piebald mule.

1st W. The good Count Sture is dead. I think of
nothing else. This demon of a king has killed him—
killed him with his own hand.

2d W. I cannot think that Lars can fancy this bloodshed.

3d W. Yes, bloodshed, bloodshed — more bloodshed.

The counselor, Burræus, is dead too. Catherine Mone
is a bad girl. My grandson Nils has broken his shoul-
der. The taxes will not let us rest. The old Gustavus
ought to come from his grave. Those were good days.
Alas, alas!

1st W. Oh, that the people could be roused to deal
with this king!

(*Exeunt.*)

ACT IV.

SCENE V. — *A room in the palace at Stockholm.*

(*Enter* ERIC *and* GORAN PERSSON.)

Eric. Embassies, embassies! Go to the pit with them
   all!
I want nothing of them or you, Goran Persson.
Avoid my presence if you do not wish
To go as Burræus did.

(*Exit* PERSSON.)

       I am a Nero —
A very Nero; I have wandered about
In the open fields and yet the skies stood firm.
I have walked the earth and yet it did not yawn
To swallow me. There is no God, or he
Would smite me dead.

       Here I have written it,
Here in my journal, under lock and key —
And the last words are

      " Counselor Persson
Is the devil in human shape. He tempts me still
To do some wicked deed and sell my soul."

(*Enter* LARS.)

Well, fool, and did you come for company?

Lars. Lift up your heart — as the old wife said when she thrashed her son. But he only lifted up his voice and wept. That is not the way to do. One ought only to weep when he has the stomach-ache, and make faces and scowl when he has a jumping tooth. For my own part, thank heaven, my mother was an ostrich and my father was a crocodile, and if you look at my jaws and legs, you will see that I tell you the truth. Some people do n't take after their parents — but that was never my way.

Eric. Come, put an end to all this silly talk!
Thou art a fool, but yet thou hast some wit.
Thou art prime minister — tell me what to do.

Lars. There is no one, my father, the crocodile, used to declare, who was more agreeable to him than a fine young woman. Now my mother, the ostrich, objected to that, but then he was accustomed to tell her that this was the way he learned wisdom, and, truly, he was embalmed after his death.

Eric. (*Aside.*) I only know one woman that I care
To see or hear, but I am cursed and stained,
.And her pure eyes would never look on me.

(*Aloud.*)

Come, fool, what woman is it that you mean?

Lars. I picked a diamond out of the mud, cousin — a diamond, I tell you, and I set it in my cap. The devil runs away now when I come near him. I am so virtuous and pious now that I do not know myself in the mirror. Martin Luther, the German, was nothing to me as a devil dispeller.

Eric. And do you mean that I should summon then
That Catherine Mone, even if I knew
That she would scorn me?

Lars. Softly, softly. They asked the ferryman if the ice was solid, and then they ventured across. Well, the bridge is firm. Go over and God keep you, and do n't forget your poor fool.

(Exit Eric.)

It is intolerable, this mask and sham,
This mummery and mockery of my life!
Only that I have thus far saved Duke John,
Only that I have thus far, now and then,
Charmed the great devil from the king's black heart,
I would away to Italy or France.
But then this Catherine, so nobly true
To God and to herself — if she might be
The guardian genius of this tortured land!
What is this Eric? Is he man or fiend?
I love him and I hate him — he is mad
And then grows sane. He murdered the good Count,
And I had murdered him, but for Duke John
And what might happen if I chanced to fail.

Why should I love the Duke or his brother Charles?
There is no tie except the grateful bond
For the rescue of my father. That is slight
As a spider's line after these months of dread.
And yet I cannot altogether leave
King Eric, till his better angel comes
To take my place.
Then — off with bells and cap!

ACT IV.

SCENE VI. — The same.

(Enter Catherine and Eric.)

Cath. Your majesty has sent to summon me.
Eric. Catherine, I have: I am the wretchedest man

That ever yet drew breath.   I loathe myself
For evil deeds — I pray, I search the stars,
I write the story out in deadly lines
Of open desperation.   Day by day
I add more words and lock the pages up.
Take pity on me — love me if you can —
For you alone I love, and if my life
Can come beneath your pure and blessed sway,
I pray you take it there and keep it safe.
I see the fires of hate in every eye;
They plot on every side to work me harm.
Oh, Catherine, have mercy on my soul !

    Cath. God must have mercy — God and the White
        Christ,
The Lord of peace, the God and Lord of love.

    Eric. Teach me to love.   I never yet have learned.
Teach me to love, by loving what I am.
God — what is God ? — You are the god I seek.

    Cath. I pray you, sire, be not so blasphemous
Against the only love that gives us love,
Without which love there is no love at all.

    Eric. Tell me its rules, then.

    Cath.   They are these : Repent,
Forgive, confess, forsake and persevere.

    Eric. What first thing must I do ?

    Cath.   Set free Duke John.

    Eric. What next ?

    Cath.   Drive evil counselors away !

    Eric. What next ?

    Cath. Stand up before the land, say, "I have sinned.
I take upon me all the shame and woe.
I was beset by devils, if you will,
But henceforth and hereafter I am free.

I make such poor repayment as I can.
I ask you, pray for me, forgive me, even
As I shall trust for mercy to my God."

Eric. Is this love's lesson, then? If such is love,
And so comes down from holy heights to man,
I have been evermore an outcast wretch,
A hateful, cruel, brutal, dreadful thing.—
The light breaks in ! It is the star, the star !
It rests upon dark waters of my soul —
Deep waters, black and sad, and there is peace !.

ACT V.

SCENE I. — *After five years. A room in the palace.*

(*Enter* LARS *and* CATHERINE.)

Lars. Fair lady, I would ask you to wink a little at
my transgressions. I want to go and eat chestnuts. If
I am missed, do you answer for me. I will leave you a
song to take away something of the blame. The country
has done well with you and me for prime ministers.
Prince John is out in the open air taking long breaths.
Goran Persson practices his algebra with a nail on a dungeon wall. It is altogether proper that while my end of
the see-saw is in the air, I should go and help some other
king. Kings need me and cry for me. Perhaps they
need me more than my Master Eric — though, now that
he is human, I could swear I love him.

Cath. We have not thanked thee as thou should'st be
    thanked,
Brave Hercules. It was not once nor twice,
In the early days of this new state of things,
That thou did'st face thy death and, with a jest,
Disarm the sentence. So have I seen a boy

Taking a humble-bee by both his wings,
Deprive him of his sting.   I never knew
What was thy secret.—

      Sometimes it was song,
Sometimes a smile, sometimes sarcastic speech,
But always most effective.

 Lars. Madam, I saw a dove, one summer day,
Chased by a hawk, and then I saw the hawk
Chased, in his turn, by such a tiny bird
That it was scarce perceptible.   So small
It seemed, I only knew its power and skill
By watching that wild hawk.   The little bird
Pecked him about the head and drove him here
And drove him there, and at the last the hawk
Was glad to fly away.   So have I done.
I sailed my ship into the tempest's eye,
I caught my swordsman underneath his guard.
I dared and so I did.   I am no fool ;
I am no jester ; but a poor, plain man,
Who loves his land and loves his king — a man
Who, when the angel came, gave up his trust,
And now, a pilgrim of the holy art
And ministry of song, goes up and down
Among the nations, singing songs of joy.
Love takes my place and holds a better rein.
Love guide you unto years of happiness !

     (Going.)

 Cath. Stay, Lars, and sing but once before you go.

 Lars. (Sings.)

    The flowers will blow,
    The skies will glow,
     The leaves will spread their green

On tree and bower
And ivied tower,
Across the land, I ween.
And many a bird
To song be stirred,
On many a tasseled spray ;
For spring draws near,
And skies are clear,
Though I am far away.

O love, dear love,
From high above,
Thy star has led me true.
O love, my light !
The darkest night
That hope has broken through.
I follow still
That lofty will ;
I watch that holy ray,
Secure and blest,
By trust and rest,
Though I am far away.

Farewell, dear madam ; if a poet's song
May prove a spell, use this.

Again, farewell!

(Going, he meets ERIC.)

Eric. Whither away, old Hercules ? I thought
I heard thee somewhere, twanging on a lute.

Lars. Perdition to all cats, I say ! There is a notable
mouser with whiskers like a Don, whose musical intes-
tines I amicably desire. I go, your majesty, to execute
justice on him without a warrant. He has an admirable
voice, but a poor method. When once I make him into
fiddle strings, he will be a delight to the sense. Farewell, farewell, as the peasant said when he gave the beg-
gar a bone.

(Exit.)

ACT V.

SCENE II. — *In John's palace.*

(*Enter* PRINCE JOHN *and* PRINCE CHARLES.)

P. John. Charles, I am out of prison, as you see.
Sture is dead — Burræus dead — the fool
Has fled away as soon as I escaped ;
The flower-girl is the favorite, so I hear.

P. Chas. Brother, one hardly dared to draw his breath
Or suffer his heart to beat. This Eric went
Raging about, a very fiend from the pit.
He killed and confiscated as he chose ;
And, in the midst of such incarnate crime,
Contrived to keep me so beyond, and out
Of any intervention, that I swore
And prayed by spasms, maddened to despair
At what the devil did in the face of God.

P. John. Now, therefore, we must lock the nobles soon
Into conspiracy, make head, revolt,
And throw this scoundrel where he once threw me.
His superstition, I have heard, is touched ;
First, by the strange departure of his fool,
And then, again, because the crown fell down.

P. Chas. Nothing I knew of that.

P. John.   Oh, yes, the crown,
It fell from the hands of him who bare it up,
Nils Gyllenstjerna, in the banquet hall.
Catherine turned pale and trembled, Eric too
Was red and white. He is not quite himself
Since Denmark's fleet was driven from our shores.
Some say it overwrought him.   .

                         Brother Charles,
Our time is short in which to gather strength.

This must be undertaken instantly.

P. Chas. I have already noticed whom to touch.
The ground is mined, the powder set; a match,
Slow-burning, is already in its place.
You do not know how much has been achieved
While you still lay in prison.

(*Exeunt.*)

ACT V.

SCENE III. — *Stockholm. The cathedral.*

(*Enter* ERIC *and a* PRIEST.)

Priest. Your majesty, the enemy advance
Without obstruction. One by one the forts
Open their gates. Your brothers, John and Charles,
Are in the van — behind them is a throng
Of nobles, peasants, burghers, miners, priests.
The word has but arrived — we pray you, haste
And arm yourself.

Eric.   I will; but conscience comes
And lays a leaden weight upon my chest.
I am pressed down to death; the mercy-drops
Of God are like that torture where the wretch,
With head bent back, half strangled, yet must feel
Drop after drop, resistless, fill his throat!
I am foredoomed! The fair-haired man, at last,
Is coming and I cannot stay his speed.
But I will die Gustavus Vasa's son!
Gird on my armor, give me my good sword,
And let the bullets tinkle as they may!

Priest. Arm! arm! They are at the gates!

(*The king rushes out of the church. At the entrance he
meets* STEN.)

Sten. Halt there !   Thou art the king !

Eric.   Put up thy pistol !

Sten. Not till thou dost yield !

Eric.   Out of my path !

Sten. Down with all tyrants !

(*Seizes him.*)

Eric. I surrender then ! I am thy prisoner.

(*Aside.*)

Caught like a rat in a trap !

ACT V.

SCENE IV. — *A hall of justice.*

(*Present:* ERIC *and the* PRINCES JOHN *and* CHARLES *and* ATTENDANTS.)

P. John. So, brother Eric, it is our turn now ;
The wheel of fortune sometimes spins about.
I make no doubt, that you will be rejoiced
To live with toads down in my hermit's cell.
When men play pitch and toss with a crown, perchance
It slips between their fingers.

P. Chas.   Oftentimes
It does so slip, and in this case it slipped.

Eric. I have no word to say, no prayer to breathe.
I do acknowledge I deserve it all.
But this I ask : Suffer me once to see
My wife before I die.

P. Chas.   His wife ! the girl
That peddled flowers upon the public street !

P. John. That was his taste, you know ; his mother's
    blood
Affected him somewhat, and now he asks
To see this woman —

Well, then, bring her in.

P. Chas. He would not do so much for you, remember.

P. John. I do remember — I remember well.

But sometimes, brother, when the cup is near,

And even grazes the lip, the wine may spill.

(*Enter* GUARD *with* CATHERINE.)

Guard. We found this woman waiting at the gate.

P. John. Is this your queenly consort, Eric ?

Eric.   Yes !

This is my wife, my angel sent from God.

P. Chas. Enough! Wrap up the angel ! send her home.

Cath. Duke John, Duke Charles ! Oh, let me speak
    one word.

I love this man ; I love him as my life.

He is not what he was — a better mind

Is in him.   Think ! Duke John, he set you free.

Duke Charles, he lifted off a heavy load

Which hung above your head.   Think of the land,

And how he governed it these latter days.

Think how, with subtle, underworking stealth,

You undermined the best that he could do.

Think how the nation prospered, and the Dane

Was driven hence defeated.

                Think of this,

And set my Eric free.   I ask no more.

And we will go to any distant land,

Or burrow in the caverns of the earth ;

Do anything, be anything, to take

The curse from off the kingdom.

P. John.   This is fine ;

Aye, this is very fine ; it pays me well

For waiting in the dungeon with the toads.

P. Chas. It pays me too, to hear such charming words

From such a lovely queen.

                        But then, but then,
One hardly finds it in his heart to free
The wolf when once he has him in the trap,
Caught by the paw, like this one.

                       Eric, Eric,
You showed good taste and prudence in your queen.
We never were presented in due form,
But now all ceremonies must be waived.

    Cath. Oh, noble lords, for God's sake, for the sake
Of him your common father; for the sake
Of the dear babe and me; for the sweet sake
Of our divine Redeemer's tenderness,
Release my Eric!

    P. John.   What is that she says?
Release her Eric — that would be, indeed,
To massacre ourselves. This is the man,
This gentle, pitiful, pathetic man,
Who made no more of cutting off a head
Than you or I in breaking off a twig.
This is the man who packed his brother down ·
In a damp, stone cask, like common butcher's meat.
This is the man who, when that gallant knight,
Count Svente Sture, stayed his hasty hand,
Beseeching mercy for that brother's life,
Smote the gray-headed count and slew him there.
This is the man — I have his private notes —
Who calls himself a Nero, and sets forth,
With horrible detail, a hundred crimes.
Should such a wretch exist?

                     No, no! He dies!

    Cath. Shall any human soul go on so far
But the Almighty may forgive its sin?

Is there a spot, above which does not stretch
The blue of everlasting space — and can
A heart, being human, pass so far from love
That there is no forgiveness with our God?
By him who truly, penitently stands
Before his Maker, stands a presence white,
With pierced hands upraised.   Then speaks a voice.
It says :   They murdered me, but I forgive.
Forgive then, as ye hope to be forgiven!
 P. Chas. That is priest's cant.   We have been juggled
  with
Like dice here in this kingdom, shaken in
And shaken out — and now it is our throw!
Take her away!
 Eric.   Farewell, my Catherine :
I richly merit all, farewell, farewell!
Oh, sin, thou art an avalanche! Farewell!
And yet, by God's help, in another world
We meet again!

    (*Exit* CATHERINE.)

 P. John.   Be silent! Hold your peace!
   (*Curtain falls.*)

ACT V.

SCENE V. — *At Orebyhus.*

Eric. (*In prison.*) How have they dragged me back
  and forth in chains!
Abo and Kastelholm and Westeras,
Stockholm and Gripsholm; now they bring me here
To Orebyhus — 'twill be over soon!
They gave me books and took them away again ;
They gave me music — took it away again.

They brought my wife where I could see her face,
And took her away again, like all the rest.
Oh, had I known in other, better days,
How I might do, as did King Olaf's Christ,
Who taught him to forgive and be forgiven,
I had not come to this dark, dreadful cell,
To these four planks — my only bed — this stool,
This table and these sullen window bars,
Which frown away the sun and chill the air.
The avalanche is on me, but I think
Even the avalanche can slide within
The deep sea of God's mercy.
      Here I sit
Deprived of even that poor, faint privilege —
The sight of wife and child, so far away
That only by a gesture could I know
If it was they or not.
     I have looked forth
To that so distant face with heavenly eyes,
And prayed for pity and for pardoning love.
O God! O God! deliver me this day
From all blood-guiltiness. Think not on the past,
For her sake who has loved me into light,
And for the sake of that White Christ, who came
For the foul leper and the desperate thief,
For the demoniac and the murderer.
Hear me, O God! and let Thy light shine in!
    (*Curtain.*)

ACT V.

SCENE VI. — *The same. Before the prison.*

(*Enter* CATHERINE *with her* CHILD *and a* JAILOR.)

Cath. Dear son, it was a dreadful journey this.
How the wolves howled! Pray God, we be not late.

Oh, sir, King Eric is my husband ; see,
Here is his signet on my finger now.
I heard that they would poison him ; may I
Address a single warning through the grate?

 Jailor. A word you may, and nothing but a word.

 Cath. I thank you, thank you. Come, my little son,
Draw near the grate and we will call his name.
Eric !

   All still.

       Eric ! Dear Eric, hear.
'Tis I, 'tis Catherine ! — Not a sound !

             Oh, sir,
Is he surely here? He is not taken hence ?

 Jailor. No ; he is here !

 Cath.   Eric ! Again, I call !
All silent ! — What was that? A groan? A groan ?
Listen ! It *is* a groan. Oh, dearest Eric !
Answer me, answer me, or I go mad !
A groan, another groan ! I heard it said
They were to give him poison in his food.
Eric, be on your guard ; they will poison you.
These bars ! these bars ! If I could tear them down !
Oh, Eric, answer !

     Groans, groans, only groans !
This is his cell and there are only groans.
He is dying and I cannot help him now !
Dying ! These groans — they are fainter, fainter still !
Now they cease altogether — not a sound.
Eric, dear Eric !

    Man, I *must* go in !
Open this gate !

 Jailor.   Madam, I dare not do it.

 Cath. Too late ! too late !

    [*Finis Tragœdiae.*]

L'ENVOI.

As the dove that the hawk would harry —
   Fair soul whom the fates pursue ! —
So Love's white wings must carry
   Such love unto me and you.

For it flies beyond chains and prison ;
   It soars above Treason's cloud —
Like a saint, from the tomb arisen,
   Deserting her mortal shroud.

And the stars look down from their distance,
   The flowers draw near with their breath,
For the love which defies resistance
   Is a Love that will conquer Death !